When I was a Grown up

And other poems

By Nichole Hansen

With illustrations by Tevin Hansen

For Elinore and Gordon

ISBN: 1941429130
ISBN-13: 978-1941429136

Poems

When I was a Grown-up

Right now you see me, and I'm so small,
But when I was a grown-up, I was very tall.
I brushed my teeth with minty paste,
And took showers with great haste.

When I was a grown-up.

When I was a grown-up, I was so tall,
That I could dunk a basketball.
And while swinging, I could go so high,
That I could almost touch the sky.

When I was a grown-up.

When I was a grown-up, I wrote books,
And fixed airplanes, and liked to cook.
I drove all around in my pink car,
And I could really play guitar.

When I was a grown-up.

When I was a grown-up, I was just like you,
And I did all the things you do.
But it was hard to be that tall,
So I decided I'd be small.

Animal Parade

There are lots of different animals,
So I'm having a parade.
I'm making all the noises,
That each one likes to say.

Cows go moo, and lions roar,
And baby chicks say peep,
But what do tall giraffes say,
When getting leaves to eat?

If monkeys ooh, ooh, ahh, ahh,
And pigs say oink a lot,
Then what do little fishies say,
When it's really hot?

The tiger gives me trouble,
Because I'm not sure what he'd say,
But I know that sheep say baaa,
And horses like to neigh.

Cats meow and ducks say quack,
And big dogs like to bark,
But what about the rhino,
Or the troublesome aardvark?

Donkeys hee and haw,
And roosters cock-a-doodle-doo,
But there are lots of animal sounds,
I don't know how to do!

Scissors

Scissors cut paper, scissors cut air,
You'll get in trouble if you use scissors . . .
. . . to cut your sister's hair.

Cars, Trucks, & Trains

Zoom, Zoom, Choo, Choo, Choo,
Vroom, Vroom, BAM!

Zoom, Zoom, Choo, Choo, Choo,
Vroom, Vroom, SLAM!

Grammi's Cookies

In her kitchen,
Just we two,
Are making something,
Just for you.

But they're so good,
So sweet and yummy,
They might all end up,
In my tummy.

Glue

He sticks to me like glue sometimes,
He never lets me be,
No matter what I'm doing,
It seems he'll never leave.

He knocks down all my towers,
He stomps on all my toys,
And all mom has to say is,
"He's such a crazy boy!"

He pulls my hair, he steals my cup,
He climbs all over me,
He sticks to me like glue sometimes,
He never lets me be.

But then . . .

He dances and he spins,
He sings a funny song,
It makes me laugh, and I spin too,
I even sing along.

He shares half-eaten crackers,
And he hugs me when I'm sad,
I guess as far as brothers go,
He's really not so bad.

So . . .

If this is what it means,
To be a family,
Then stuck together like glue sometimes,
Is the perfect way to be.

Stinky Brothers

Oh, the stinky stuck-up boys,
They never let me in,
To their super smelly clubhouse,
Where they toot and burp and grin.

It's my horrid heinous brother,
And his hideous hairy friends,
They just sit up there laughing,
They never let me in!

I really don't know what they do,
In that revolting rancid place,
It's just a repulsive hovel,
Where they stare right into space.

My friends, we have tea and cakes,
In my sweet and saccharine circle,
We wear royal regal gowns,
And jewels that shine and sparkle.

We never toot, we never burp,
We never stare right into space,
Like stinky stuck-up boys,
In their super smelly place.

The Best in the Whole Wide World

Do you want to be the best,
The best in the whole wide world?
Then listen to the words I say,
And write down all I've told.

First you'll need some purple,
And then you'll need some pink,
Throw in lots of shiny,
And a little fluff, I think.

It never hurts to dance a bit,
And sing a lovely song,
And if you sing it loud enough,
Then all can sing along.

Smiles are good, but hugs are better,
Just take a look and see,
To be the best in the whole wide world,
You mostly act like me.

Pippin

Pippin, Pippin, took so long,
That little Pippin sang a song.
It started as a gentle hum,
Then grew louder 'til he was done.

Pippin, Pippin, was in no rush,
To see the swirling, twirling flush.
He just sang and tapped his toes,
Waiting patiently to go.

Pippin wanted to delay,
Naptime on this Saturday.
He had better things to do,
Like read a book or twenty-two.

Then Pippin's mum said to her son,
"Two more minutes and you're done!"
He didn't whine or try to fight,
Just washed his hands and said, "Goodnight."

Rain

Rain, rain, come my way,
I'm feeling very hot today.
I need some puddles, right away!
So rain, rain, please come my way.

Leftover Tuesday

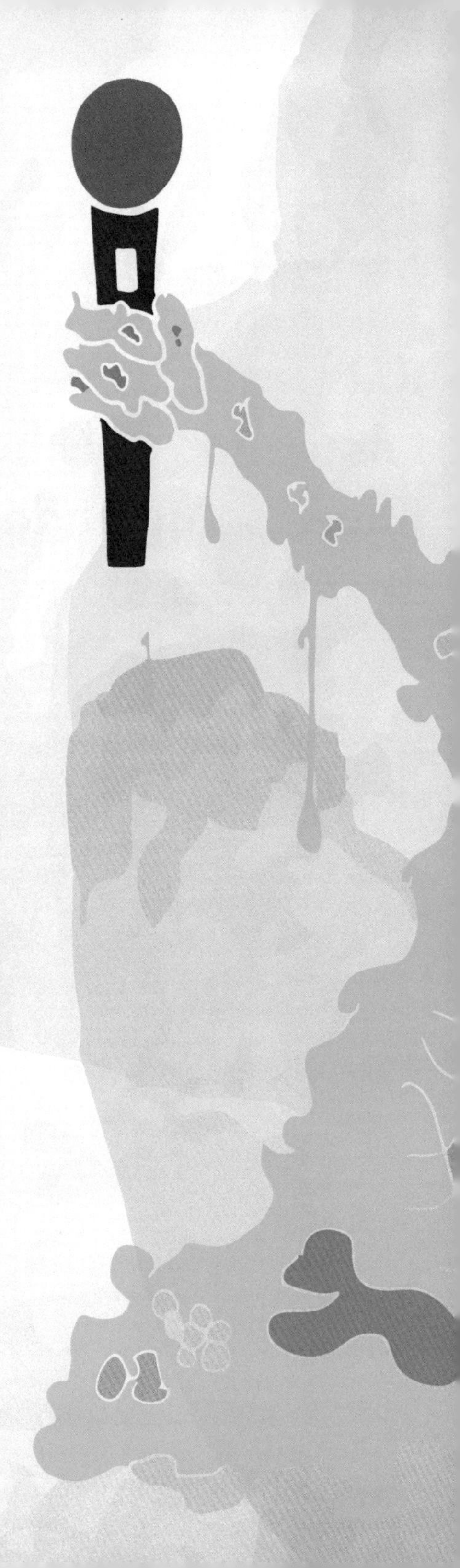

Mom was quite surprised today,
When she opened up the door.
Things weren't what she expected,
In our refrigerator.

It looked a little fuzzy,
It was growing green and grey,
I think it started as the meatloaf,
That we had sometime in May.

It was dipping the ketchup,
And jiving with the juice.
It was sashaying by the lettuce,
In a brand new three cheese suit.

What it was we couldn't say,
Mom said, "It's just not right."
And now we eat leftovers,
Every Tuesday night!

I hear the little fuzzy guy,
Has found himself a job.
He sings songs in Vegas now,
With the Incredible Jello Blob.

Things to Do

Things to do, things to do,
It's hard finding things to do.

When dad is talking on the phone,
He says, "You'll have to wait."
But I don't want to play with cars,
And I don't want to paint.

Things to do, things to do,
It's hard finding things to do.

When mom is making supper,
She says, "Be patient, please!"
But she's been cooking forever,
And it's only mac 'n' cheese!

Things to do, things to do,
It's hard finding things to do.

Dust Bunnies

We read a book, I had a snack,
Then dad sang me a song,
Mom tucked in my covers,
But something was quite wrong.

I heard a noise beneath my bed,
And when I took a peek,
Sixteen eyes, all in a row,
Were staring back at me.

I yelled for mom, but she just sighed,
Dad said, "Now, just stop stalling!"
But when I was carried off, they knew,
Dust bunnies had come calling.

Goodbye

Goodbye for now, and tout a l'heure,
(That's French for toodaloo).
It's time to say, right now, for sure,
This book is truly through.

Made in the USA
Lexington, KY
02 October 2018